Dear Parent:
Your child's love of reading starts here!

Every child learns to read in a different way and at his or her own speed. Some go back and forth between reading levels and read favorite books again and again. Others read through each level in order. You can help your young reader improve and become more confident by encouraging his or her own interests and abilities. From books your child reads with you to the first books he or she reads alone, there are I Can Read Books for every stage of reading:

SHARED READING
Basic language, word repetition, and whimsical illustrations, ideal for sharing with your emergent reader

BEGINNING READING
Short sentences, familiar words, and simple concepts for children eager to read on their own

READING WITH HELP
Engaging stories, longer sentences, and language play for developing readers

READING ALONE
Complex plots, challenging vocabulary, and high-interest topics for the independent reader

ADVANCED READING
Short paragraphs, chapters, and exciting themes for the perfect bridge to chapter books

I Can Read Books have introduced children to the joy of reading since 1957. Featuring award-winning authors and illustrators and a fabulous cast of beloved characters, I Can Read Books set the standard for beginning readers.

A lifetime of discovery begins with the magical words "I Can Read!"

Visit www.icanread.com for information
on enriching your child's reading experience.

For Owen Anastas,
a dazzling reader
—J.O'C.

For my dazzling *friend*
Sue Littman
—R.P.G.

For P.S., who saw the
potential joy contained
in a rainbow pack of
construction paper
—T.E.

HarperCollins®, 📖®, and I Can Read Book® are trademarks of HarperCollins Publishers.

Fancy Nancy: The Dazzling Book Report
Text copyright © 2009 by Jane O'Connor
Illustrations copyright © 2009 by Robin Preiss Glasser
All rights reserved. Manufactured in China.
No part of this book may be used or reproduced in any manner whatsoever without written permission except in the case of brief quotations embodied in critical articles and reviews. For information address HarperCollins Children's Books, a division of HarperCollins Publishers, 10 East 53rd Street, New York, NY 10022.
www.icanread.com

Library of Congress Cataloging-in-Publication Data
O'Connor, Jane.
The dazzling book report / by Jane O'Connor ; cover illustration by Robin Preiss Glasser ; interior illustrations by Ted Enik. — 1st ed.
p. cm. — (Fancy Nancy) (I can read! Level 1)
Summary: Nancy is determined to make the cover of her very first book report as fancy as she can, but she spends so much time on it that she has no time to write about the book.
ISBN 978-0-06-170368-3 (pbk.) — ISBN 978-0-06-170369-0 (trade bdg.)
[1. Homework—Fiction. 2. Schools—Fiction. 3. Vocabulary—Fiction.] I. Preiss-Glasser, Robin, ill. II. Enik, Ted, ill. III. Title.
PZ7.O222Daz 2009   2008024646
[E]—dc22   CIP
                                                                                                                        AC

12 13 14 SCP 10 9 8 7 6 5
❖
First Edition

I Can Read!

BEGINNING 1 READING

Fancy NANCY

The Dazzling Book Report

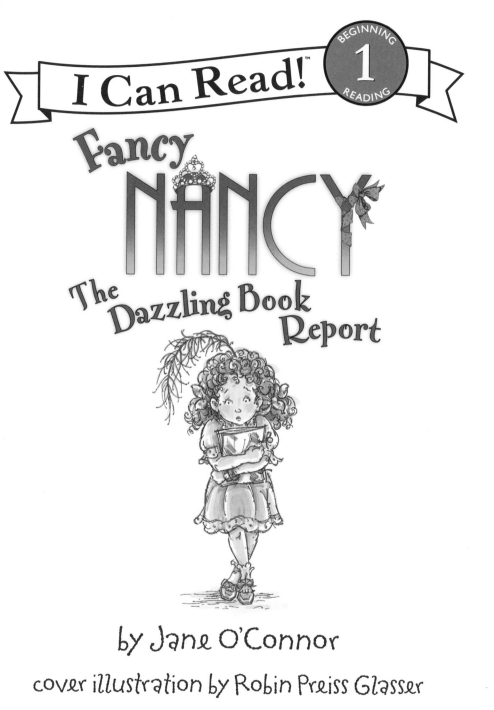

by Jane O'Connor

cover illustration by Robin Preiss Glasser

interior illustrations by Ted Enik

HarperCollins*Publishers*

Monday is my favorite day.

Why?

Monday is Library Day.

Before we leave, we select a book.

(Select is a fancy word for pick.)

It is like getting a present

for a week!

Bree selects a book on dinosaurs.

Robert selects a book
of funny poems.

Teddy selects a scary story.

I select a book
about an Indian girl.
She has a fancy name,
Sacajawea.
You say it like this:
SACK-uh-jah-WAY-ah.

Later Ms. Glass has

thrilling news.

(Thrilling is even more exciting

than exciting.)

We get to do a book report!

"Your first book report.

How grown up!"

my mom says at dinner.

10

"Yes, I know," I say.

"My book is a biography.

It is about a real person."

After dinner I read my book.

Dad helps with the hard words.

I learn all about Sacajawea.

Sacajawea was a princess.

She lived two hundred years ago

out West.

She helped two explorers

reach the Pacific Ocean.

Mom takes me to the art store.

I need stuff for

the cover of my book report.

I want it to be great!

(I am the second-best artist
in our class.
This isn't bragging.
You can ask anybody.)

I get a bag of little beads,

some yarn,

and markers.

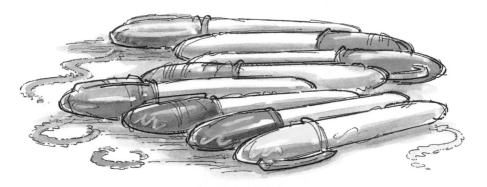

I start working on the cover.

I work on it every night.

I make Sacajawea look very brave,

because she was.

She found food for the explorers.

She kept them safe from enemies.

"Just remember to
leave time for the words,"
Mom keeps saying.
"I will. I will," I tell her.

"Ms. Glass wants you
to write about the book,"
Dad says over and over.
"That's what a report is."
"I know that!" I tell him.
Writing the words will be easy.

Ta-da! The cover is finished.

Sacajawea has yarn braids.

Beads and fringe are glued

on her clothes.

I must admit it is dazzling.

(That is fancy for eye-popping.)

Now I will write my report.

I get out lined paper

and a pen with a plume.

(That's a fancy word for feather.)

The trouble is, I am tired.

I know all about Sacajawea.

But the right words won't come.

What am I going to do?

I have to hand in my report tomorrow!

"I am desperate!" I tell Mom.

(That means I'm in trouble.)

Mom lets me stay up longer.
Still my report ends up
only two sentences long.

The next day,

everyone sees my cover

and says, "Wow!"

But hearing other reports
makes me nervous.
All of them are longer
than mine.
All of them are more interesting.

I read my report.

"Sacajawea was a heroine.

She helped people in trouble."

Everybody waits to hear more.

But there is no more.

I am crestfallen.

(That is fancy for sad and ashamed.)

"I spent too much time
on the cover,"
I tell Ms. Glass.

Ms. Glass understands.

"Why don't you tell the class about your book?"

So I do.

I tell them all about

the brave things Sacajawea did.

Sacajawea was a heroine.

Ms. Glass is a heroine too.

At least, she is to me!

Fancy Nancy's Fancy Words

These are the fancy words in this book:

Biography—a story about a real person

Crestfallen—sad and ashamed

Dazzling—eye-popping, a knockout

Desperate—feeling trapped

Heroine—a girl or a woman who is brave and helps people

Plume—feather

Select—to pick

Thrilling—even more exciting than exciting